AB 17.00

GLENN PIANO BY GLADYS PRIDDIS

Glenn Piano
by Gladys Priddis

Jason Dickson

BookThug | Toronto
Department of Narrative Studies No. 3

FIRST EDITION
copyright © 2010 Jason Dickson

Published by BookThug with generous assisstance from
the Canada Council for the Arts and The Ontario Arts
Council.

 Canada Council   Conseil des Arts
for the Arts   du Canada

 ONTARIO ARTS COUNCIL
CONSEIL DES ARTS DE L'ONTARIO

All rights reserved. No part of this publication may be
reproduced or transmitted in any form or by any means,
electronic or mechanical, including photocopying,
recording, or any information storage or retrieval system,
without permission in writing from the publisher.

Printed in Canada.

LIBRARY AND ARCHIVES CANADA
CATALOGUING IN PUBLICATION

Dickson, Jason, 1977-
  Glenn Piano by Gladys Priddis / Jason Dickson.

ISBN 978-1-897388-53-2

  I. Title.

PS8607.I34G63 2010   C813'.6   C2010-900536-8

ONE

At the end of her life, Gladys Priddis wanted to tell the story of Glenn Piano, how she came to know him, how she came to live with him, and of the charges of murder that were brought against him, as well as herself, charges she believed were false.

I had the opportunity to interview her during her later years, when she was a patient at Victoria Hospital. What follows is a record of her story, at times told directly in her own words, with the appropriate biographical and historical facts included.

Gladys Priddis was born in London, Ontario, the daughter of a doctor. She was educated at Hellmuth Ladies College, and worked as a seamstress. Before meeting her husband Jonathan Priddis, she lived in a small apartment over a jewellery store on Richmond Street. She met her husband at party on Christmas Eve. He was a young barrister, and they were eventually married.

"Our life was simple, and he adored me. We were blessed with a quiet marriage." A degeneration in Jonathan's left eye, however, made him partly blind at the age of twenty-five – first in the left eye, and finally in the right, so that he could no longer practice law.

He was fortunate to know many doctors, and Gladys became his attendant, learning from them how to take care of his disease. But without work, and with no time for her to make money, their funds dwindled to a fraction of their former size. This was in 1887. Her spells began shortly after.

Gladys had nervous shocks. Jonathan's condition was getting worse, and in her state, she found it more difficult to treat him. It was decided that she also find help from a doctor, but not official help, as they could no longer afford it. She needed someone who was more homeopathic about nervous disturbances, and Dr. Piano came recommended by a friend.

Piano had studied somewhere in Europe and had made a name for himself in Montreal before coming to London. Gladys did not know that the mind could be studied, but she trusted her husband and his friend, who knew more about this than she did.

"I walked to his house alone, since Jonathan was too sick to accompany me. On the outside, his house appeared bland. It was Victorian, mildly ornate, and spacious. However inside, it was a pioneer home, with equipment nailed to the walls, raw furniture, and an atmosphere of discovery."

"At the back there was a two floor operating theatre accessible from a door off of the hall. It had plain pine seats arranged along the wall and a table used for surgery. The rest of the room was dissecting tables on trestles – with a pot of water and surgical instruments boiling on the stove."

She did not know how many animals lived there, although she always saw one moving, and was no longer sure whether they were from there or somewhere else. There was an odour of agriculture that came from the back, although the house also smelled, appropriately, of medicine.

As for Piano himself, he was a small man, nearly bald, with a stoop and little glasses. "He carried himself like a briefcase." One of the first things she noticed was that he was exceptionally well dressed.

Their sessions went well. Gladys was an attentive patient. Piano was a good doctor. She talked about her spells, and he listened, writing things down. She was calmed by the visits. It was new not to feel sick, or rather, to feel that her sickness was understood. Something could be done.

It came to be so that when she was out for a walk at night she often passed by his house, hoping that he'd see her and invite Jonathan and her to dinner — which he eventually did, with a table expertly set when they arrived. The blinds were opened up "and a phonograph played Sweet Marie, I believe."

"Piano, in his simple way, told us stories of his travels to India, South America and the Orient. I was enchanted."

The two became better acquainted as their sessions continued. It was Mrs. Priddis at first, and remained so until several months into their sessions, when Piano began addressing her by her first name. The sessions were professional but informal. But in the winter of 1888 it was decided by Jonathan, Piano, and Gladys that a more immediate measure should be taken if she was to get well.

They scheduled an operation for the following month, with Gladys being given a temporary room in Piano's house to properly prepare and recover. Jonathan was allowed to be with them during the operation, although he could not help, and sat only to the side in a chair – it was enough to ease his mind that he was doing what he could. The operation only required minor exploration, and they were assured that it was not dangerous.

"Shortly after he placed me under I heard boots at the garrison. I recognized the sound of marching on the garrison ground because I slept to it in my old house, the house where I lived with my father, and sometimes I was awake and heard the call of soldiers at their practice, when my house was a block away. I did not know what they were doing, what they were trying to do, and as the knife cut into my scalp, I heard them again."

"The soldiers all left the garrison grounds, July 1868, leaving an empty field flecked with a few abandoned military buildings. I visited the grounds soon after and found bottles near the old mess hall and bone from the cows that grazed there. The field became Victoria Park. And I remembered how the lights lit up in Victoria Park when I watched from the bedroom that night it opened – a supernatural display of yellow bulbs with new hydro."

TWO

There was a small, weather-beaten garden at the rear of Piano's property that Gladys found to be a relaxing place to visit, shaded on one side by a hedge, and sloping southward to the river. It was a place to reflect on herself, "to view myself in an impartial manner."

"My husband and I used to walk to the Thames River at night along the paths. We often visited Springbank Park as it was being built." Gladys often thought of Jonathan's love for her during her time in Piano's garden. She thought of how special he was, of how she should feel lucky that he was her husband.

As Piano learned more about Jonathan's health he became interested in him as a potential patient. Perhaps Piano might see something that the other doctors could not? Gladys trusted Piano, and she convinced her husband to come with her to see him. "Jonathan agreed to let Piano operate on his eye, as long as I was there as well. And it was suggested that I be Piano's assistant in the operation, after some training, of course."

"We performed the first operation – one of three – and Piano said that it was a success. Jonathan was given a room on the second floor in which to recover. We were hopeful."

Gladys was such a good assistant that Piano asked her to help him in other surgeries. "I became Piano's assistant, and partly recovered by watching the doctor work. The rows of medicaments, each placed carefully out on the shelves, fascinated me. Stocked Cinchona or Peruvian bark, zinc in the form of pills, charcoal powder, arsenic, and opium. I used iron, strychnine, and electricity."

Gladys lit the lamps and held the thongs. She was

the exterminator of noxious draughts. She held the hands of the ill as they tried to recover. "Once, without any anaesthetic, I helped Piano incise the abdomen of a local merchant, removing a portion of the omentum, and took out the cavity, all without a single sterile technique."

But Gladys' skills could do nothing to save Jonathan. His condition declined, and he died in his room in the Winter of 1889. Gladys grieved, and refused to stay at her old house, staying that night in her room at Piano's, sleeping in a grey light until morning.

Jonathan and Gladys were bankrupt. So Piano offered her full-time position as his assistant. Gladys agreed, and was very thankful. Piano seemed charitable, holy. Perhaps he could help her become healthy again, to eventually find a life, even without her husband?

Piano put much thought into when Gladys' second operation was to be held. He explained to her that he had found, through many years of experience, that the time of day one operated had an effect on his patient's recovery. Afternoons were the least desirable time, "although, admittedly, if one needed to operate then — if it was an emergency — then one did not have a choice." Evening was best, for he explained that a quiet meditation came over him after dark which improved his skills as a surgeon.

Gladys was laid out on the table and told to relax, to think of an empty, open space, and describe it — a process that made her sleepy. When Piano gave the anaesthetic, she remembered her father being shot at the Richmond Tavern.

"I remember people taking him to the doctor's house where they dragged him in and set him down on a wood table. The room was lit with lanterns. The doctor stood over him with a knife pushed into his stomach, trying to find the bullet. 'I need something smaller,' he said to the others, and looked at me. I was pulled to the table where the doctor grabbed my hand and pushed it into my father's stomach, 'In there,' the doctor said, 'Find the bullet.'"

"I didn't know about surgery then, and only felt liquid and organs, and knew nothing about where to find the bullet. I remember that I was crying, because I believed that finding the bullet would keep my father alive, and the thought of him dying brought me to tears. The doctor stared down at me, holding the lamp, and did not give instructions. And he was right because I suddenly put my finger against something hard and carefully dragged it into two fingers and out through the organs and into my hand."

Gladys' father was kept in the east wing of Victoria Hospital, and she visited him daily. He was dear to her. And she had saved his life.

She found it strange to see him lying sick on a bed. Gladys did not understand what had happened, or what was happening then, though she tried. She looked into him and saw a father who loved her, and night and day passed, possibly for the first time. She refused to leave and stayed beside him.

There Gladys had thoughts, or rather the inclination of thoughts, as she woke and slept beside her father, as the scenes of hospital life played out around them. He died shortly afterward, while she was asleep.

"After that I spoke little and let others speak over me. I made myself available to be written upon with clothes and ideas, so that it only pleased me when I pleased others. I ate the food of my family, walked their routes, and celebrated their victories. At night, I prayed at the edge of my bed for their safety, quietly feeling a dread beneath my prayers that they all might one day disappear."

"People corrected me. My instincts were unsound. Each outfit that I had to wear was adjusted to fit my frame. My gait was unbalanced, necessarily morbid. Every flash of regeneration in me, such as a desire to play music or be a doctor, was extinguished immediately by those in charge. As a result, there has always remained beneath my grace a feverish altercation of wants. My blessed time is punctured by alternating dreams."

"I was a palimpsest with my desires."

She could hardly admit it to herself at the time, but there was a distinct euphoria in being diseased. Mostly at night, when she lay awake in her bedroom, there came an unbelievable peace of mind. "I was balanced, ensured". The knowledge of her state was comprehensible for the first time in her life. It had been declared and was solidly understood that she was unwell, and whenever Gladys doubted her motives, her habits, or her mind, she could easily think, "You are unwell, and this will all be over, sooner or later." Knowing this was the first thing she was certain of in her life.

THREE

Poems of Gladys Priddis

A common misunderstanding of water is that it is still. How many times, Piano, have you encountered a picture of a lake on a wall and knew that it was meant to calm you? I've never found too much pleasure in this illusion.

A lake always moves. It is filled with too much not to move. As the wind and moon lash from above, and the core of the earth pushes up from below, so moves a lake. Though they are often quiet and peacefull if you're on the shore, underneath and inside of them life moves with celerity. And if we were to look into their depth, we would see, mirrored in its

body, a shape like the heart.
For like a lake, the heart too moves with creatures of its own. It makes in itself the inventory of a life. And like a bird coming up for air, it longs to throw itself into the open. Is this longing not the exact opposite of stillness?

Water boils. It needs heat, for it cannot boil on its own. But given heat, like anything else, water will surely change.

In this way, water is like the ways that one's love can change. Not forever! Certainly not. It can alter from one form to the next, and then back, if needed — the love of friends, of family, of lovers.

Like how the materials of the world turn from gas, to steam, turn solid.

In the unstoppable friction of the world, the heart and its love change shape. It is as if the heart itself

is the friction of the world,
the energy that is made
from what is outside of
the body touching what
is in.

Whoever rises or falls into
each other like heated water,
the result is a love that is
restive. It is always
moving, like the sound of
hushed, hurried voices,
of wild Aeolian harps—
a song, amatory and
desirous.

Water falls from the sky and collects in small pools on the lane beside your house. It ornaments the drive and lights the lane that leads up to your door.

Remember how bright everything looks after a storm? Does the world ever seem like this any other time? Even under an overcast sky, the rainy landscape shines through a dark and dense palate of colour. Looking at these small pools collected near your house, I think of how the world seems altered, as if blood has rushed to the surface of its face.

I think of how your own face changes colour. When you blush, to me your face is made wondrous with the movement beneath it. Your skin is the landscape of your heart, flushed with blood.

I always hope that my body on yours inspires a colour like the water that collects on the lane in front of your house. I want to leave a colour that is luminous, drawn from you, rushing up through your veins to the lip of your skin, to meet

my kiss on its pink and
wet surface.

Drops of water are most extraordinary and rare, for they do not stay, but instead turn into pools of water. Only in rain, after rain, or in instances of natural or human design, such as a spout, can one watch and study this special form.

Drops of water are rare for they exist as water in transition, water moving from one place to the next, from one shape to another. They can move quickly, like how they fall from a leaf after a storm. Or they can move slowly, like how a drop of water takes its time to move across a tilted window.

Piano, I have a desire to be a drop of water that has fallen on your skin, a droplet that has a will to move where it pleases, to reach places in you that I am otherwise unable to reach, or a drop that does not have a will, and is bound to the movements of your body.

I appear, contact, and cover your surface, I can see, magnified beneath, the beautifull details of your skin. Think, Piano, what I could do if I covered you.

Water covers whatever surface it can find. In this respect, a lover is a pool of water, surrounding the other with a covering surface. Here I think of appearing at your door, and without a sound, touch your feet, then your left leg,
Your right leg,
Your waist,
Your hands,
Your arms,
Your neck,
and the rest. For a moment all of the sounds in the room disappear, and we are inside something indescribable.
At this point, you open your eyes and look into

the water. You notice how the light in the room changes in this depth. The colours look like the innumerable pigments that are found in your skin — my skin?

What does it matter?

It is said that drowning is the most peaceful way to die, that after the initial panic, a state of euphoria occurs where the closing moments of your life are collect and still. I think that it explains much of what we find attractive about love.

For as lovers soon found out, there is an oppressive weight that must be carried with love. This weight takes on many shapes: absence, distance, fear, and frequently the opposite, denseness, imminence, certainty. One often hears of people drowning in love, as if it were a death, an end, under a lonely and affecting water.

But just as the oblivion of death is somehow naturally attractive, in that it is mysterious, final, and consuming, so is our attraction to the weight of love. For who can really resist the burden that it places? It seems as though the body is made for it, that it has, inside of itself, a way of making the burden bearable, like a peaceful swimmer who has lost their way at the bottom of the sea.

And like death in water, the burden of love can escape the horrific ends that wait for so many who are dry and, as a consequence, enclosed by land. Love can become a forfeit to the certainty of death's embrace, the decadent but certain last rites of life. In this way, I love you becomes a call to a handsome and human end in the arms of another, at the bottom of the sea, sated, like a swimmer lost, who still sings of their life, who dies in the body of another— la petite mort.

Piano, I look out into the world like someone who sees the sky from underwater. It is strange, but I rarely feel as though my hand reaches the surface of things, let alone penetrate into whatever lies beneath.

Yet I am the sky. I am the rain. The rain fallen. My body is made from the very materials that elude me. I feel the friction of heat and the still of cold. I am the result, the esoteric form, realized by my life.

When I am with you, and my body is laid into the folds of my bed,

these forms rise up in me
like constellations. And
though I cannot see or
touch them, I sense their
movement from one side of
the sky to the other.
  They leave a coat of
sweat on my skin.
A mouth full of syrup,
A hand that is wet,
A body rising.
  And meeting you in the
folds of my bed, I can
almost reach the surface
of things, and like a cup
that has tilted over, let
water run from my body
onto yours.

Strangely, in all the weight of love, the ultimate result, at times, is lightness — a cleansing of worry and uncertainty. Like how the roughest surface, when under water, becomes a smooth and beautifull object.

Love turns the most discomfited heart into a jewel.

When I fell in love with you, Piano, my heart lost a specific weight. It threw itself out of me (to be picked up and carried) and now moves, hidden, as a lit resident of your body. It is almost as if

my heart became part of
you (how do I explain?)
that your body, when
pressed up against me,
your body moving
outside in the world is,
in part, the movement
of my heart on the earth.

And how can we speak of water without speaking of the absence of water? Is it here that our metaphor will reveal its most illuminating detail? For as the body is the architect of love, then it follows that without water, love desiccates.

It is most clearly a consumption of sorts, to love, that a body's appetite is in part the desire to eat and drink from the body of another. Without this feast of bodies, love cannot be. Without it, the lips dry. The body weakens. The craft of love cracks like a cup.

When we are together, time slows to such a rate that I can see it. The details of our time island, and I can discern and see into it ways otherwise unknown to me. Only when I think of you, Piano, can I achieve anything like it.

When you leave in the morning, your absence is immediately felt. My day appears to me in the form of a certain and limited amount of time, as if I am preparing for a fast. I do my work. I make food and entertain myself. I am often happy.

Sometimes, often in the

middle of the day, Piano, my body aches.

FOUR

The small Italian boy was brought to Piano's house on the evening of March 3rd, 1890. He was the son of a bankrupt Italian merchant who once had a shop off Adelaide Street. The boy was blind from a tumour that had grown on his eye, and Piano had agreed to remove it.

Gladys did not know that a boy would be that evening's patient. When she entered the operating theatre the sight of him on the table surprised her. He was asleep, as Piano had already given him a dose of ether, and after Gladys approached the table, Piano began the operation.

Gladys was in charge of organizing the medical instruments, which she did carefully on a tray to the left. She handed him the instruments and watched uneasily as the boy's tumour was peeled away, taking with it the eye and much of the skin.

She felt compelled to do everything she could. The operation was a success, and Gladys bandaged him and helped Piano take him upstairs where he would recover.

Afterward, Gladys and Piano sat together in his office and waited for the boy to sleep off the anaesthetic. "We've done a good thing tonight," Piano said. And it was then that Gladys knew that her doctor was one of the most remarkable men she had ever met. "How could one not think this after experiencing such a thing?"

The next day Gladys woke and rushed downstairs to see the boy. But all she found was Piano in the theatre, cleaning his equipment. The boy is in his room, he said, and wasn't to be disturbed. Gladys spent the day in the garden, recalling the previous night.

Weeks passed, and only once did she see him – in the front entry walking up to the landing – and then nothing. Piano said that the operation was a success, and the boy had been returned to his family. Gladys felt good, but also sad. She had wanted to see the boy at least once before he went home.

She began to look in the streets for him whenever she was out. He still lived off of Adelaide, as his father had found a job in one of the factories there. Perhaps his mother might take him along Dundas Street if she were buying groceries?

The afternoons in that area were busy, and Gladys stalled in the shops to look for him, before returning home. Her plan was to introduce herself to his mother, to explain that she had assisted in the operation, and to see the boy, saying, "He looks as though he is doing quite fine."

She did see a one-eyed boy in the area begging for money at the corner of Dundas and Adelaide, but he did not look like the Italian boy. His face had not been damaged. This boy stood quietly holding out his hat as the people passed, and Gladys thought of going over and giving him some money, although she didn't for some reason.

It was after one of these strolls in early evening that Gladys came home to find Piano sitting in the dark front room, smoking his pipe. From the hall, she could see the dark room and the orange light of his match and clearly thought that she could distinguish a shape move in the chair beside him. "Are we having a guest tonight," she asked, and he replied curtly that he was alone. "The sound of a chair rocking was heard, and I was sure that a sound came from the room behind him, but all that I could see was the light from his smoke and the dark."

The next night, after she had swept the second floor landing in front of her room, she saw the back of a dark-haired woman moving around the corner towards the attic steps. She searched the house for the next three hours, finding Piano in his laboratory and asking him about it, but found no one.

"I didn't see her until a few nights later when, in the middle of my sleep, I awoke to see myself knelt at the edge of my bed."

The woman appeared the next night at Piano's table. She sat quietly, and Piano hardly spoke to her. The dinner was tense, as she never looked at Gladys. Later Gladys saw her standing by his office door in the front entry. She watched as Gladys passed, and did not say a word, and Gladys didn't speak to her either, asking only to be let by.

"She thought that any part of my life was hers to invade. Wherever I went in the house there was always the possibility that she would be there. She slept in the hall sometimes, just outside of my door. Where else was I to go? The only place where she was not there was outside, or into the country, and even then I could still sense her. She had even begun to sleep in the room where Jonathan once slept."

One night, Gladys was getting ready for dinner when Piano called for her to come down. She still needed a minute to prepare, but hurried, knowing he'd call up again. She sat down at the table and tried to ignore the smell of the food. The woman came in again and sat down at the table. Piano acknowledged her before Gladys, and Gladys threw her plate at the wall and ran out of the house.

"How sudden our actions can be!"

Gladys ran to Piano's garden, but it did not calm her. She ran passed the Thames, to Springbank Park. "But even there things imposed themselves on me." The posts had been marked for the construction of the ferry dock, and Gladys swam out to one of them, climbing onto it, "in order to feel some kind of escape."

Gladys later wrote: "My fever is like a shadow cast onto my body. It moves when I move, but it cannot be reached or moved on its own. It is only encountered, like how the dusk creeps up on you, suddenly appearing when only one light is left, but appearing inward, like a veil passing over the eyes, or a cloud entering the room from a door. I don't know. I don't know what I am trying to say."

It became clear to Piano and Gladys that they would have to try something drastic if Gladys was to lead a normal life. They planned the third operation for the next full moon, a night said by Piano to have unique medical powers.

Gladys prepared herself in her bedroom, placing each of her items on the bureau, and fixing her hair up in a bun. The clock struck midnight in the hall, giving the signal that she was to leave her old room and go to the operation theatre, where Piano was waiting.

She spread herself out onto the table without hesitation, unlike before, when she could hardly breathe. Piano marked the places of incision on her forehead with a pen. A record was played, Sweet Marie, Gladys recalls, and this time Piano didn't speak, just simply let the record play so she would slowly fall asleep. But she opened her eyes after he made the first incision, and saw him looking down at her, and she wept.

"I remembered walking with my father along the Thames River one night, thinking of how frightening it looked in the dark. What of the horrible things that lie at the bottom of lakes? What sickening objects do you think would surface if we were to drain all the water away?"

"We travelled with torches and spells back then, to ward off the mosquitoes, as any bite would send fever to the brain. Near London there was more rot than life, as any moment spent in the woods would tell you. It was a cheerless village."

Gladys was found early the next morning lying in the centre of Dundas and Richmond Streets, wearing her night-gown, face in the dirt. An open cut around her fore-head had hardened in the mud. She was taken to Victoria Hospital where she was treated for severe blood loss, eye trauma, and poison.

The investigation focused mainly on Dr. Piano. But it also included Gladys as his accomplice. It was claimed that Piano had murdered a small Italian boy, first blinding him, and then bleeding him to death. It was said that he had operated on and killed a Mr. Jonathan Priddis, leaving his wife, Gladys Priddis, a penniless widow, desperate and insane.

But what did they know, Gladys insisted? "That Piano has helped so many people? I can think of at least a dozen souls saved by his good work. And because he did not work in a hospital they must judge him like a criminal."

"He was all the hope that these sick people had in the world."

Gladys died in the hospital, shortly after my interview.

FIVE

Coda

Jonathan told me that our house was an island in the city. To enter it was like leaving for another place.

He described me in loving detail, with a romantic embellishment that I found both charming and childish.

He said that when he passed my house it was on fire. At other times, it was underwater. That he could feel it in his skin.

Each night, after we retired, Jonathan would spend

himself pouring out his heart to me, cradling me in his arms, and wording his love with an exactness that was almost apprehensible.

But in spite of my charitable attitude to him, despite my indulgence of this ritual, I was embarrassed by his descriptions. They were common, and he was blind.

To hear these words come from a blind person made me miserable.

At first Jonathan seemed like a helpless child and I wanted to protect him.

But after our marriage, I felt only distance.

For some unnamable reason, I need to be seen by my lover in order for love to return.

Why do I need to be seen?

When he knows me so well, when I am such a central subject in his life, why is the thought that he will never see me so uncomfortable?

Why does he fail in my heart?

It is because there will always be a place in him that is inaccessible. That place is somehow in his eyes, a dark that is incomprehensible in its blindness.

I cannot even find the darkest room in this black house in which to understand him.

And although I partly love him more than I can stand, there has always, and will always be, this space where he is no longer mine, where he is bafflingly and frighteningly himself.

He tries to communicate this place to me, in gasps at night, through meaningless gestures and distance.

He reaches out to me with his hands, his arms that I see are part of him – eyes or no eyes – that are fundamentally my husband and no other, but that will forever contain an empty place that I can never reach, a place of absence.

I have found that a lover needs somewhere in which to disappear, and what was most identifiable in

Jonathan was never mine to enter.

Instead, in the final years of our marriage, I found myself drawn to Piano's house despite the love for my husband.

I was drawn not by love but to somehow vanish into its rooms.

And I did, often, sit and disappear, after the night came, waking in the morning, although I didn't sleep.

I saw things in the dark that were not imaginable in the day, parts of my life told and retold, things I'd forgotten.

I found myself, and in myself I found that I could endure an unlikely amount of solitude and doubt.

For in the morning, after I came out from the dark, the halls had cleared in the grey light, and Piano's house was the image of a place that I could inhabit.

And there moved in me new recollections of a home that I could had never imagined before.

Acknowledgements

The author acknowledges the support of the
Ontario Arts Council in the writing of this book.

Jason Dickson lives in Bracebridge Ontario where he owns and operates the Muskoka Bookhouse. He is the author of two previous titles: *Clearance: The Selected Journals of Dr Michael Purdon, Parapsychologist* and *The Hunt,* both of which were published by BookThug.

Colophon

Manufactured in an edition of 500 copies in the spring of 2010 by BookThug | Distributed in Canada by the Literary Press Group www.lpg.ca | Distributed in the United States by Small Press Distribution www.spdbooks.org | Shop on-line at www.bookthug.ca

Type + design by Jay MillAr
The Department of Narrative Studies is edited
  for the press by Jenny Sampirisi.
Calligraphy by Diannah Benson
Cover image: *Cicuta maculate* (Water Hemlock)